The ANIMALS of FARMER JONES

By Leah Gale • Pictures by Richard Scarry

A GOLDEN BOOK, New York
Western Publishing Company, Inc.
Racine, Wisconsin 53404

This edition of one of the earliest and most popular of all Little Golden Books has been specially illustrated by Richard Scarry, one of the most popular of Little Golden Book artists.

It is supper time on the farm.
The animals are very hungry.
But where is Farmer Jones?

The horse stamps in his stall.
"Nei-g-hh, nei-g-hh," says the horse.

"I want my supper."
But where is Farmer Jones?

The cow jangles her bell.
"Moo, moo," says the cow.
"I am very hungry."
But where is Farmer Jones?

The sheep sniff around the barn.
"Ba-a-a, ba-a-a-a," say the sheep.
"We're waiting for supper."
But where is Farmer Jones?

"Cluck, cluck," say the chickens.
"Give us our supper."
But where is Farmer Jones?

The turkey fluffs his feathers.
"Gobble, gobble," says the turkey.
"My food! My food!"
But where is Farmer Jones?

The ducks waddle out of the pond.
"Quack, quack," say the ducks.
"Supper time, supper time."
But where is Farmer Jones?

The dog runs about barking.
"Wuff, wuff," says the dog.
"I want my meal."
But where is Farmer Jones?

The cat rubs against a post.
"Me-o-w, me-o-w," says the cat.
"My dish is empty."
But where is Farmer Jones?

The pigs snuffle in the trough.
"Oink, oink," say the pigs.
"There's nothing to eat."
But where is Farmer Jones?

Farmer Jones is out in the field.

"Six o'clock!" says Farmer Jones.

"It's supper time!"

He goes to get food for the animals.

He gives oats to the horse.
"Nei-g-hh, nei-g-hh," says the horse.
"Thank you, Farmer Jones."

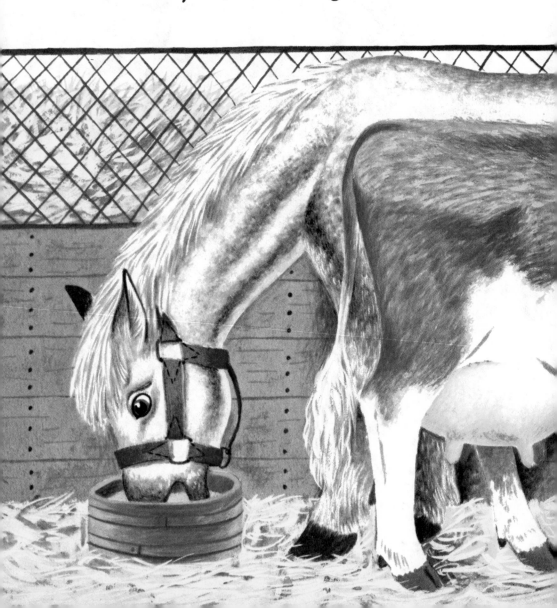

He gives grain to the cow.

"Moo, moo," says the cow.

"Thank you, Farmer Jones."

He gives turnips to the sheep.
"Ba-a-a, ba-a-a-a," say the sheep.
"Thank you, Farmer Jones."

He gives corn to the chickens.
"Cluck, cluck," say the chickens.
"Thank you, Farmer Jones."

He gives wheat to the turkey.
"Gobble, gobble," says the turkey.
"Thank you, Farmer Jones."

He gives barley to the ducks.

"Quack, quack," say the ducks.

"Thank you, Farmer Jones."

He gives bones to the dog.
"Wuff, wuff," says the dog.
"Thank you, Farmer Jones."

He gives milk to the cat.

"Me-e-o-w, me-e-o-w," says the cat.

"Thank you, Farmer Jones."

He gives mash to the pigs.

"Oink, oink," say the pigs.

"I am hungry, too," says Farmer Jones.

And off he goes for his supper.